FREAKS

BY

TOD ROBBINS

British Library Cataloguing-in-Publication Data
A catalogue record for this book is available from the
British Library

CONTENTS

TOD ROBBINS

Clarence Aaron 'Tod' Robbins was born in Brooklyn, New York in 1888. During his youth he had a somewhat conflicting interest in both athletics in poetry, and at Washington and Lee University was both editor of the year book and captain of the track team at the same time. Shortly after graduating, Robbins inherited a large amount of money, and found himself financially independent. In 1909, he caused something of a scandal in Brooklyn by eloping with Edith Norman Hyde, who would later win the first 'Miss America' title. In spite of being short-lived, the marriage produced two sons.

In 1917, after two largely unnoticed novels and a poetry collection, Robbins published what is now his most famous work, *The Unholy Three*. The novel recounts the strange criminal misadventures of three refugees from a circus – Tweedledum the dwarf, Hercules the giant and Echo the ventriloquist. It was twice adapted for the screen, in 1925 as a silent version directed by Tod Browning, and in 1930 as a sound version directed by Jack Conway. Six years after *The Unholy Three*, in 1923, *Munsey's Magazine* published 'Spurs', the short story which Tod Browning used as the basis of his notorious 1932 cult horror film *Freaks*. Shortly afterwards, lifelong Francophile Robbins moved to the French Riviera with his third (of an eventual four) wives, where he divided his time between writing and playing tennis. However, this leisurely life was brought to an abrupt end by the onset of World War II. When the Nazis invaded, Robbins refused to leave France, and spent the war in a concentration camp, surviving the ordeal but dying not long afterwards.

Robbins is largely forgotten today; apart from 'Spurs', most of his writings have been out of print for over half a century. Some critics see this as a great shame, and regard Robbins as an important writer in the canons of horror and mystery fiction.

FREAKS

TOD ROBBINS

*

1

JACQUES COURBÉ was a romanticist. He measured only twenty-eight inches from the soles of his diminutive feet to the crown of his head; but there were times, as he rode into the arena on his gallant charger, St. Eustache, when he felt himself a doughty knight of old about to do battle for his lady.

What matter that St. Eustache was not a gallant charger except in his master's imagination—not even a pony, indeed, but a large dog of a nondescript breed, with the long snout and upstanding ears of a wolf? What matter that Monsieur Courbé's entrance was invariably greeted with shouts of derisive laughter and bombardments of banana skins and

3

orange peel? What matter that he had no lady and that his daring deeds were severely curtailed to a mimicry of the bareback riders who preceded him? What mattered all these things to the tiny man who lived in dreams and who resolutely closed his shoe-button eyes to the drab realities of life?

The dwarf had no friends among the other freaks in Copo's Circus. They considered him ill-tempered and egotistical, and he loathed them for their acceptance of things as they were. Imagination was the armour that protected him from the curious glances of a cruel, gaping world, from the stinging lash of ridicule, from the bombardments of banana skins and orange peel. Without it, he must have shrivelled up and died. But these others? Ah, they had no armour except their own thick hides! The door that opened on the kingdom of imagination was closed and locked to them; and although they did not wish to open this door, although they did not miss what lay beyond it, they resented and mistrusted anyone who possessed the key.

Now it came about, after many humiliating performances in the arena, made palatable only by dreams, that love entered the circus tent and beckoned commandingly to Monsieur Jacques Courbé. In an instant the dwarf was engulfed in a sea of wild, tumultuous passion.

Mademoiselle Jeanne Marie was a daring bareback rider. It

made Monsieur Jacques Courbé's tiny heart stand still to see her that first night of her appearance in the arena, performing brilliantly on the broad back of her aged mare, Sappho. A tall, blonde woman of the amazon type, she had round eyes of baby blue which held no spark of her avaricious peasant's soul, carmine lips and cheeks, large white teeth which flashed continually in a smile, and hands which, when doubled up, were nearly the size of the dwarf's head.

Her partner in the act was Simon Lafleur, the Romeo of the circus tent—a swarthy, Herculean young man with bold black eyes and hair that glistened with grease like the back of Solon, the trained seal.

From the first performance Monsieur Jacques Courbé loved. Mademoiselle Jeanne Marie. All his tiny body was shaken with longing for her. Her buxom charms, so generously revealed in tights and spangles, made him flush and cast down his eyes. The familiarities allowed to Simon Lafleur, the bodily acrobatic contacts of the two performers, made the dwarf's blood boil. Mounted on St. Eustache, awaiting his turn at the entrance, he would grind his teeth in impotent rage to see Simon circling round and round the ring, standing proudly on the back of Sappho and holding Mademoiselle Jeanne Marie in an ecstatic embrace, while she kicked one shapely bespangled leg skyward.

"Ah, the dog!" Monsieur Jacques Courbé would mutter.

"Some day I shall teach this hulking stable-boy his place! *Ma foi*, I will clip his ears for him!"

St. Eustache did not share his master's admiration for Mademoiselle Jeanne Marie. From the first he evinced his hearty detestation for her by low growls and a ferocious display of long, sharp fangs. It was little consolation for the dwarf to know that St. Eustache showed still more marked signs of rage when Simon Lafleur approached him. It pained Monsieur Jacques Courbé to think that his gallant charger, his sole companion, his bedfellow, should not also love and admire the splendid giantess who each night risked life and limb before the awed populace. Often, when they were alone together, he would chide St. Eustache on his churlishness.

"Ah, you devil of a dog!" the dwarf would cry. "Why must you always growl and show your ugly teeth when the lovely Jeanne Marie condescends to notice you? Have you no feelings under your tough hide? Cur, she is an angel and you snarl at her! Do you not remember how I found you, a starving puppy in a Paris gutter? And now you must threaten the hand of my princess! So this is your gratitude, great hairy pig!"

Monsieur Jacques Courbé had one living relative—not a dwarf, like himself, but a fine figure of a man, a prosperous farmer living just outside the town of Roubaix. The elder Courbé had never married and so one day, when he was found dead from heart failure, his tiny nephew—for whom, it must be confessed, the farmer had always felt an instinctive aversion—fell heir to a comfortable property. When the tidings were brought to him, the dwarf threw both arms about the shaggy neck of St. Eustache and cried out:

"Ah, now we can retire, marry and settle down, old friend! I am worth many times my weight in gold!"

That evening, as Mademoiselle Jeanne Marie was changing her gaudy costume after the performance, a light tap sounded on the door.

"Enter!" she called, believing it to be Simon Lafleur, who had promised to take her that evening to the Sign of the Wild Boar for a glass of wine to wash the sawdust out of her throat. "Enter, *mon chéri!*"

The door swung slowly open and in stepped Monsieur Jacques Courbé, very proud and upright, in the silks and laces of a courtier, with a tiny gold-hilted sword swinging at his hip. Up he came, his shoe-button eyes all a-glitter to see the more than partially revealed charms of his robust lady. Up he came to within a yard of where she sat, and down on one knee he went and pressed his lips to her red-slippered foot.

"Oh, most beautiful and daring lady," he cried, in a voice as shrill as a pin scratching on a window-pane, "will you not take mercy on the unfortunate Jacques Courbé? He is hungry for your smiles, he is starving for your lips! All night long he tosses on his couch and dreams of Jeanne Marie!"

"What play-acting is this, my brave little fellow?" she asked, bending down with the smile of an ogress. "Has Simon Lafleur sent you to tease me?"

"May the black plague have Simon!" the dwarf cried, his eyes seeming to flash blue sparks. "I am not play-acting. It is only too true that I love you, mademoiselle, that I wish to make you my lady. And now that I have a fortune, now that—" He broke off suddenly and his face resembled a withered apple. "What is this, mademoiselle?" he said, in the low, droning tone of a hornet about to sting. "Do you laugh at my love? I warn you, mademoiselle—do not laugh at Jacques Courbé!"

Mademoiselle Jeanne Marie's large, florid face had turned purple from suppressed merriment. Her lips twitched at the corners. It was all she could do not to burst out into a roar of laughter.

Why, the ridiculous little manikin was serious in his love-making! This pocket-sized edition of a courtier was proposing marriage to her! He, this splinter of a fellow, wished to make her his wife! Why, she could carry him about on her shoulder like a trained marmoset!

What a joke this was—what a colossal, corset-creaking joke! Wait till she told Simon Lafleur! She could fairly see him throw back his sleek head, open his mouth to its widest dimensions and shake with silent laughter. But *she* must not laugh—not now. First she must listen to everything the dwarf had to say, draw all the sweetness out of this bonbon of humour before she crushed it under the heel of ridicule.

"I am not laughing," she managed to say. "You have taken me by surprise. I never thought, I never even guessed—"

"That is well, mademoiselle," the dwarf broke in. "I do not tolerate laughter. In the arena I am paid to make laughter, but these others pay to laugh at *me*. I always make people pay to laugh at me!"

"But do I understand you aright, Monsieur Courbé? Are you proposing an honourable marriage?"

The dwarf rested his hand on his heart and bowed. "Yes. mademoiselle, an honourable marriage, and the wherewithal to keep the wolf from the door. A week ago my uncle died and left me a large estate. We shall have a servant to wait on our wants, a horse and carriage, food and wine of the best, and leisure to amuse ourselves. And you? Why, you will be a fine lady! I will clothe that beautiful big body of yours with silks and laces! You will be as happy, mademoiselle, as a cherry tree in June!"

The dark blood slowly receded from Mademoiselle Jeanne Marie's full cheeks, her lips no longer twitched at the corners, her eyes had narrowed slightly. She had been a bareback rider for years and she was weary of it. The life of the circus tent had lost its tinsel She loved the dashing Simon Lafleur, but she knew well enough that this Romeo in tights would never espouse a dowerless girl.

The dwarf's words had woven themselves into a rich mental tapestry. She saw herself a proud lady, ruling over a country estate, and later welcoming Simon Lafleur with all the luxuries that were so near his heart. Simon would be overjoyed to marry into a country estate. These pygmies were a puny lot. They died young! She would do nothing to hasten the end of Jacques Courbé. No, she would be kindness itself to the poor little fellow, but, on the other hand, she would not lose her beauty mourning for him.

"Nothing that you wish shall be withheld from you as long as you love me, mademoiselle," the dwarf continued. "Your answer?"

Mademoiselle Jeanne Marie bent forward and, with a single movement of her powerful arms, raised Monsieur Jacques Courbé and placed him on her knee. For an ecstatic instant she held him thus, as if he were a large French doll, with his tiny sword cocked coquettishly out behind. Then she planted on his cheek a huge kiss that covered his entire face from chin to brow.

"I am yours!" she murmured, pressing him to her ample bosom. "From the first I loved you, Monsieur Jacques Courbé!"

2

The wedding of Mademoiselle Jeanne Marie was celebrated in the town of Roubaix, where Copo's Circus had taken up its temporary quarters. Following the ceremony, a feast was served in one of the tents, which was attended by a whole galaxy of celebrities.

The bridegroom, his dark little face flushed with happiness and wine, sat at the head of the board. His chin was just above the tablecloth, so that his head looked like a large orange that had rolled off the fruit-dish. Immediately beneath his dangling feet, St. Eustache, who had more than once evinced by deep growls his disapproval of the proceedings, now worried a bone with quick, sly glances from time to time at the plump legs of his new mistress. Papa Copo was on the dwarf's right, his large round face as red and benevolent as a harvest moon. Next him sat Griffo, the giraffe boy, who was covered with spots, and whose neck was so long that he looked down on all the rest, including Monsieur Hercule Hippo, the giant. The rest of the company included Mademoiselle Lupa, who had sharp white teeth of an incredible length, and who growled when she tried to talk, the tiresome Monsieur Jejongle, who insisted on juggling fruit, plates and knives, although the whole company was heartily sick of his tricks; Madame Samson, with her trained baby boa constrictors coiled about her neck and peeping out timidly, one above each ear; Simon Lafleur and a score of others.

The bareback rider had laughed silently and almost continually ever since Jeanne Marie had told him of her engagement. Now he sat next to her in his crimson tights. His black hair was brushed back from his forehead and so glistened with grease that it reflected the lights overhead, like a burnished helmet. From time to time he tossed off a brimming goblet of Burgundy, nudged the bride in the ribs with his elbow and threw back his sleek head in another silent outburst of laughter.

"And you are sure that you will not forget me, Simon?" she whispered, "It may be some time before I can get the little ape's money."

"Forget you, Jeanne?" he muttered. "By all the dancing devils in champagne, never! I will wait as patiently as Job till you have fed that mouse some poisoned cheese. But what will you do with him in the meantime, Jeanne? You must allow him no liberties. I grind my teeth to think of you in his arms!"

The bride smiled and regarded her diminutive husband with an appraising glance. What an atom of a man! And yet life might linger in his bones for a long time to come. Monsieur Jacques Courbé had allowed, himself only one glass of wine and yet he was far gone in intoxication. His tiny face was suffused with blood and he stared at Simon Lafleur belligerently. Did he suspect the truth?

"Your husband is flushed with wine!" the bareback rider whispered. "*Ma foi, madame*, later he may knock you about! Possibly he is a dangerous fellow in his cups. Should he maltreat you, Jeanne, do not forget that you have a protector in Simon Lafleur."

"You clown!" Jeanne Marie rolled her large eyes roguishly and laid her hand for an instant on the bareback rider's knee. "Simon, I could crack his skull between my finger and thumb, like this hickory nut!" She paused to illustrate her example, and then added reflectively: "And, perhaps, I shall do that very thing, if he attempts any familiarities. Ugh! The little ape turns my stomach!"

By now the wedding guests were beginning to show the effects of their potations. This was especially marked in the case of Monsieur Jacque's associates in the side-show.

Griffo, the giraffe boy, had closed his large brown eyes and was swaying his small head languidly above the assembly, while a slightly supercilious expression drew his lips down at the corners. Monsieur Hercule Hippo, swollen out by his libations to even more colossal proportions, was repeating over and over: "I tell you I am not like other men. When I walk, the earth trembles!" Mademoiselle Lupa, her hairy upper lip lifted above her long white teeth, was gnawing at a bone, growling unintelligible phrases to herself and shooting savage, suspicious glances at her companions. Monsieur Jejongle's hands had grown unsteady and, as he insisted on juggling the knives and plates of each new course, broken bits of crockery littered the floor. Madame Samson, uncoiling her necklace of baby boa constrictors, was feeding them lumps of sugar soaked in rum. Monsieur Jacques Courbé had finished his second glass of wine and was surveying the whispering Simon Lafleur through narrowed eyes.

There can be no genial companionship among great egotists who have drunk too much. Each one of these human oddities thought that he or she alone was responsible for the crowds that daily gathered at Copo's Circus; so now, heated with the good Burgundy, they were not slow in asserting themselves. Their separate egos rattled angrily together, like so many pebbles in a bag. Here was gunpowder which needed only a spark.

"I am a big—a very big man!" Monsieur Hercule Hippo said sleepily. "Women love me. The pretty little creatures leave their pygmy husbands, so that they may come and stare at Hercule Hippo of Copo's Circus. Ha, and when they return home, they laugh at other men always! 'You may kiss me again when you grow up', they tell their sweethearts."

"Fat bullock, here is one woman who has no love for you!" cried Mademoiselle Lupa, glaring sidewise at the giant over

15

her bone. "That great carcass of yours is only so much food gone to waste. You have cheated the butcher, my friend. Fool, women do not come to see *you*! As well might they stare at the cattle being led through the street. Ah, no, they come from far and near to see one of their own sex who is not a cat!"

"Quite right," cried Papa Copo in a conciliatory tone, smiling and rubbing his hands together. "Not a cat, mademoiselle, but a wolf. Ah, you have a sense of humour! How droll!"

"I *have* a sense of humour," Mademoiselle Lupa agreed, returning to her bone, "and also sharp teeth. Let the erring hand not stray too near!"

"You, Monsieur Hippo and Mademoiselle Lupa, are both wrong," said a voice which seemed to come from the roof. "Surely it is none other than me whom the people come to stare at!"

All raised their eyes to the supercilious face of Griffo, the giraffe boy, which swayed slowly from side to side on its long, pipe-stem neck. It was he who had spoken, although his eyes were still closed.

"Of all the colossal impudence!" cried the matronly Madame Samson. "As if my little dears had nothing to say on the subject!" She picked up the two baby boa constrictors, which lay in drunken slumber on her lap, and shook them like whips at the wedding guests. "Papa Copo knows only too well that it is on account of these little charmers, Mark Antony and Cleopatra, that the side-show is so well attended!"

The circus owner, thus directly appealed to, frowned in perplexity. He felt himself in a quandary. These freaks of his were difficult to handle. Why had he been fool enough to come to Monsieur Jacques Courbé's wedding feast? Whatever he said would be used against him.

As Papa Copo hesitated, his round, red face wreathed in ingratiating smiles, the long deferred spark suddenly alighted in the powder. It all came about on account of the carelessness of Monsieur Jejongle, who had become engrossed in the conversation and wished to put in a word for himself. Absent-mindedly juggling two heavy plates and a spoon, he said in a petulant tone : "You all appear to forget *me*!"

Scarcely were the words out of his mouth when one of the heavy plates descended with a crash on the thick skull of Monsieur Hippo, and Monsieur Jejongle was instantly remembered. Indeed, he was more than remembered, for the giant, already irritated to the boiling-point by Mademoiselle Lupa's insults, at this new affront struck out savagely past her and knocked the juggler head-over-heels under the table.

Mademoiselle Lupa, always quick-tempered and especially so when her attention was focused on a juicy chicken bone, evidently considered her dinner companion's conduct far from decorous and promptly inserted her sharp teeth in the offending hand that had administered the blow. Monsieur Hippo, squealing from rage and pain like a wounded elephant, bounded to his feet, overturning the table.

Pandemonium followed. Every freak's hands, teeth, feet, were turned against the others. Above the shouts, screams, growls and hisses of the combat, Papa Copo's voice could be heard bellowing for peace:

"Ah, my children, my children! This is no way to behave! Calm yourselves, I pray you! Mademoiselle Lupa, remember that you are a lady as well as a wolf!"

There is no doubt that Monsieur Jacques Courbé would have suffered most in this undignified fracas had it not been for St. Eustache, who had stationed himself over his tiny master and who now drove off all would-be assailants. As it was, Griffo, the unfortunate giraffe boy, was the most defenceless and therefore became the victim. His small, round head swayed back and forth to blows like a punching bag. He was bitten by Mademoiselle Lupa, buffeted by Monsieur Hippo, kicked by Monsieur Jejongle, clawed by Madame Samson, and nearly strangled by both the baby boa constrictors, which had wound themselves about his neck like hangmen's nooses. Undoubtedly he would have fallen a victim to circumstances had it not been for Simon

Lafleur, the bride and half a dozen of her acrobatic friends, whom Papa Copo had implored to restore peace. Roaring with laughter, they sprang forward and tore the combatants apart.

Monsieur Jacques Courbé was found sitting grimly under a fold of the tablecloth. He held a broken bottle of wine in one hand. The dwarf was very drunk and in a towering rage. As Simon Lafleur approached with one of his silent laughs, Monsieur Jacques Courbé hurled the bottle at his head.

"Ah, the little wasp!" the bareback rider cried, picking up the dwarf by his waistband. "Here is your fine husband, Jeanne! Take him away before he does me some mischief. *Parbleu*, he is a bloodthirsty fellow in his cups!"

The bride approached, her blonde face crimson from wine and laughter. Now that she was safely married to a country estate she took no more pains to conceal her true feelings.

"Oh, *la, la*!" she cried, seizing the struggling dwarf and holding him forcibly on her shoulder. "What a temper the little ape has! Well, we shall spank it out of him before long!"

"Let me down!" Monsieur Jacques Courbé screamed in a paroxysm of fury. "You will regret this, madame! Let me down, I say!"

But the stalwart bride shook her head. "No, no, my little one!" she laughed. "You cannot escape your wife so easily! What, you would fly from my arms before the honeymoon!"

"Let me down!" he cried again. "Can't you see that they are laughing at me?"

"And why should they not laugh, my little ape? Let them laugh, if they will, but I will not put you down. No, I will carry you thus, perched on my shoulder, to the farm. It will set a precedent which brides of the future may find a certain difficulty in following!"

"But the farm is quite a distance from here, my Jeanne," said Simon Lafleur. "You are as strong as an ox and he is only a marmoset, still, I will wager a bottle of Burgundy that you set him down by the roadside."

"Done, Simon!" the bride cried, with a flash of her strong white teeth. "You shall lose your wager, for I swear that I could carry my little ape from one end of France to the other!"

Monsieur Jacques Courbé no longer struggled. He now sat bolt upright on his bride's broad shoulder. From the flaming peaks of blind passion he had fallen into an abyss of cold fury. His love was dead, but some quite alien emotion was rearing an evil head from its ashes.

"So, madame, you could carry me from one end of France to the other!" he droned in a monotonous undertone. "From one end of France to the other! I will remember that always, madame!"

"Come!" cried the bride suddenly. "I am off. Do you and the others, Simon, follow to see me win my wager."

They all trooped out of the tent. A full moon rode the heavens and showed the road, lying as white and straight through the meadows as the parting in Simon Lafleur's black, oily hair. The bride, still holding the diminutive bridegroom on her shoulder, burst out into song as she strode forward. The wedding guests followed. Some walked none too steadily. Griffo, the giraffe boy, staggered pitifully on his long, thin legs. Papa Copo alone remained behind.

"What a strange world!" he muttered, standing in the tent door and following them with his round blue eyes. "Ah, these children of mine are difficult at times—very difficult!"

3

A year had rolled by since the marriage of Mademoiselle Jeanne Marie and Monsieur Jacques Courbé. Copo's Circus had once more taken up its quarters in the town of Roubaix. For more than a week the country people for miles around had flocked to the side-show to get a peep at Griffo, the giraffe boy; Monsieur Hercule Hippo, the giant; Mademoiselle Lupa, the wolf lady; Madame Samson, with her baby boa constrictors; and Monsieur Jejongle, the famous juggler. Each was still firmly convinced that he or she alone was responsible for the popularity of the circus.

Simon Lafleur sat in his lodgings at the Sign of the Wild Boar. He wore nothing but red tights. His powerful torso, stripped to the waist, glistened with oil. He was kneading his biceps tenderly with some strong-smelling fluid.

Suddenly there came the sound of heavy, laborious footsteps on the stairs. Simon Lafleur looked up. His rather gloomy expression lifted, giving place to the brilliant smile that had won for him the hearts of so many lady acrobats.

"Ah, this is Marcelle!" he told himself. "Or perhaps it is Rose, the English girl; or, yet again, little Francesca, although she walks more lightly. Well, no matter—whoever it is, I will welcome her!"

But now the lagging, heavy footfalls were in the hall and,

a moment later, they came to a halt outside the door. There was a timid knock.

Simon Lafleur's brilliant smile broadened. "Perhaps some new admirer who needs encouragement," he told himself. But aloud he said: "Enter, mademoiselle!"

The door swung slowly open and revealed the visitor. She was a tall, gaunt woman dressed like a peasant. The wind had blown her hair into her eyes. Now she raised a large, toil-worn hand, brushed it back across her forehead and looked long and attentively at the bareback rider.

"You do not remember me?" she said at length.

Two lines of perplexity appeared above Simon Lafleur's Roman nose; he slowly shook his head. He, who had known so many women in his time, was now at a loss. Was it a fair question to ask a man who was no longer a boy and who had lived? Women change so in a brief time! Now this bag of bones might at one time have appeared desirable to him.

Parbleu! Fate was a conjurer! She waved her wand and beautiful women were transformed into hags, jewels into pebbles, silks and laces into hempen cords. The brave fellow who danced tonight at the prince's ball might tomorrow dance more lightly on the gallows tree. The thing was to live and die with a full belly. To digest all that one could—that was life!

"You do not remember me?" she said again.

Simon Lafleur once more shook his sleek, black head. "I have a poor memory for faces, madame," he said politely. "It is my misfortune, when there are such beautiful faces."

"Ah, but you should have remembered, Simon!" the woman cried, a sob rising up in her throat. "We were very close together, you and I. Do you not remember Jeanne Marie?"

"Jeanne Marie!" the bareback rider cried. "Jeanne Marie, who married a marmoset and a country estate? Don't tell me, madame, that you—"

He broke off and stared at her, open-mouthed. His sharp black eyes wandered from the wisps of wet, straggling hair down her gaunt person till they rested at last on her thick cowhide boots, encrusted with layer on layer of mud from the countryside.

"It is impossible!" he said at last.

"It is indeed Jeanne Marie," the woman answered, "or what is left of her. Ah, Simon, what a life he has led me! I have been merely a beast of burden! There are no ignominies which he has not made me suffer!"

"To whom do you refer?" Simon Lafleur demanded. "Surely you cannot mean that pocket edition husband of yours—that dwarf, Jacques Courbé?"

"Ah, but I do, Simon! Alas, he has broken me!"

"He—that toothpick of a man?" the bareback rider cried,

with one of his silent laughs. "Why, it is impossible! As you once said yourself, Jeanne, you could crack his skull between finger and thumb like a hickory nut!"

"So I thought once. Ah, but I did not know him then, Simon! Because he was small, I thought I could do with him as I liked. It seemed to me that I was marrying a manikin. 'I will play Punch and Judy with this little fellow,' I said to myself. Simon, you may imagine my surprise when he began playing Punch and Judy with me!"

"But I do not understand, Jeanne. Surely at any time you could have slapped him into obedience!"

"Perhaps," she assented wearily, "had it not been for St. Eustache. From the first that wolf dog of his hated me. If I so much as answered his master back, he would show his teeth. Once, at the beginning, when I raised my hand to cuff Jacques Courbé, he sprang at my throat and would have torn me limb from limb had not the dwarf called him off. I was a strong woman, but even then I was no match for a wolf!"

"There was poison, was there not?" Simon Lafleur suggested.

"Ah, yes, I, too, thought of poison, but it was of no avail. St. Eustache would eat nothing that I gave him and the dwarf forced me to taste first of all food that was placed before him and his dog. Unless I myself wished to die, there was no way of poisoning either of them."

"My poor girl!" the bareback rider said, pityingly. "I begin to understand, but sit down and tell me everything. This is a revelation to me, after seeing you stalking homeward so triumphantly with your bridegroom on your shoulder. You must begin at the beginning."

"It was just because I carried him thus on my shoulder that I have had to suffer so cruelly," she said, seating herself on the only other chair the room afforded. "He has never forgiven me the insult which he says I put upon him. Do you remember how I boasted that I could carry him from one end of France to the other?"

"I remember. Well, Jeanne?"

"Well, Simon, the little demon has figured out the exact distance in leagues. Each morning, rain or shine, we sally out of the house—he on my back, the wolf dog at my heels—and I tramp along the dusty roads till my knees tremble beneath me from fatigue. If I so much as slacken my pace, if I falter, he goads me with his cruel little golden spurs, while, at the same time, St. Eustache nips my ankles. When we return home, he strikes so many leagues off a score which he says is the number of leagues from one end of France to the other. Not half that distance has been covered and I am no longer a strong woman, Simon. Look at these shoes!"

She held up one of her feet for his inspection. The sole of the cowhide boot had been worn through; Simon Lafleur caught a glimpse of bruised flesh caked with the mire of the highway.

"This is the third pair that I have had," she continued hoarsely. "Now he tells me that the price of shoe leather is too high, that I shall have to finish my pilgrimage barefooted."

"But why do you put up with all this, Jeanne?" Simon Lafleur asked angrily. "You, who have a carriage and a servant, should not walk at all!"

"At first there was a carriage and a servant," she said, wiping the tears from her eyes with the back of her hand, "but they did not last a week. He sent the servant about his business and sold the carriage at a near-by fair. Now there is no one but me to wait on him and his dog."

"But the neighbours?" Simon Lafleur persisted. "Surely you could appeal to them?"

"We have no near neighbours, the farm is quite isolated. I would have run away many months ago if I could have escaped unnoticed, but they keep a continual watch on me. Once I tried, but I hadn't travelled more than a league before the wolf dog was snapping at my ankles. He drove me back to the farm and the following day I was compelled to carry the little fiend till I fell from sheer exhaustion."

"But tonight you got away?"

"Yes," she said, with a quick, frightened glance at the door. "Tonight I slipped out while they were both sleeping and came here to you. I knew that you would protect me, Simon, because of what we have been to each other. Get Papa Copo to take me back in the circus and I will work my fingers to the bone! Save me, Simon!"

Jeanne Marie could no longer suppress her sobs. They rose in her throat, choking her, making her incapable of further speech.

"Calm yourself, Jeanne," Simon Lafleur said soothingly. "I will do what I can for you. I shall have a talk with Papa copo tomorrow. Of course, you are no longer the same woman that you were a year ago. You have aged since then, but perhaps our good Papa Copo could find you something to do."

He broke off and eyed her intently. She had stiffened in the chair, her face, even under its coat of grime, had gone a sickly white.

"What troubles you, Jeanne?" he asked a trifle breathlessly.

"Hush!" she said, with a finger to her lips. "Listen!"

Simon Lafleur could hear nothing but the tapping of the rain on the roof and the sighing of the wind through the trees. An unusual silence seemed to pervade the Sign of the Wild Boar.

"Now don't you hear it?" she cried with an inarticulate gasp. "Simon, it is in the house—it is on the stairs!"

At last the bareback rider's less sensitive ears caught the

sound his companion had heard a full minute before. It was a steady *pit-pat, pit-pat*, on the stairs, hard to dissociate from the drip of the rain from the eaves, but each instant it came nearer, grew more distinct.

"Oh, save me, Simon, save me!" Jeanne Marie cried, throwing herself at his feet and clasping him about the knees. "Save me! It is St. Eustache!"

"Nonsense, woman!" the bareback rider said angrily, but nevertheless he rose. "There are other dogs in the world. On the second landing there is a blind fellow who owns a dog. Perhaps it is he you hear."

"No, no—it is St. Eustache's step! My God, if you had lived with him a year, you would know it, too! Close the door and lock it!"

"That I will not," Simon Lafleur said contemptuously. "Do you think I am frightened so easily? If it is the wolf dog, so much the worse for him. He will not be the first cur I have choked to death with these two hands!"

Pit-pat, pit-pat—it was on the second landing. *Pit-pat, pit-pat*—now it was in the corridor, and coming fast. *Pit-pat*—all at once it stopped.

There was a moment's breathless silence and then into the room trotted St. Eustache. Monsieur Jacques Courbé sat astride the dog's broad back, as he had so often done in the circus ring. He held a tiny drawn sword, his shoe-button eyes seemed to reflect its steely glitter.

The dwarf brought the dog to a halt in the middle of the room and took in, at a single glance, the prostrate figure of Jeanne Marie. St. Eustache, too, seemed to take silent note of it. The stiff hair on his back rose up, he showed his long white fangs hungrily and his eyes glowed like two live coals.

"So I find you *thus*, madame!" Monsieur Jacques Courbé said at last. "It is fortunate that I have a charger here who can scent out my enemies as well as hunt them down in the open. Without him, I might have had some difficulty in discovering you. Well, the little game is up. I find you with your lover!"

"Simon Lafleur is not my lover!" she sobbed. "I have not seen him once since I married you until tonight! I swear it!"

"Once is enough," the dwarf said grimly. "The impudent stable-boy must be chastised!"

"Oh, spare him!" Jeanne Marie implored. "Do not harm him, I beg of you! It is not his fault that I came! I—"

But at this point Simon Lafleur drowned her out in a roar of laughter.

"Ho, ho!" he roared, putting his hands on his hips. "You would chastise me, eh? *Nom d'un chien!* Don't try your circus tricks on *me*! Why, hop-o-my thumb, you who ride on a dog's back like a flea, out of this room before I squash you!

Begone, melt, fade away!" He paused, expanded his barrel-like chest, puffed out his cheeks and blew a great breath at the dwarf. "Blow away, insect," he bellowed, "lest I put my heel on you!"

Monsieur Jacques Courbé was unmoved by this torrent of abuse. He sat very upright on St. Eustache's back, his tiny sword resting on his tiny shoulder.

"Are you done?" he said at last, when the bareback rider had run dry of invectives. "Very well, monsieur! Prepare to receive cavalry!" He paused for an instant, then added in a high, clear voice: "Get him, St. Eustache !"

The dog crouched and, at almost the same moment, sprang at Simon Lafleur. The bareback rider had no time to avoid him and his tiny rider. Almost instantaneously the three of them had come to death grips. It was a gory business.

Simon Lafleur, strong man as he was, was bowled over by the wolf dog's unexpected leap. St. Eustache's clashing jaws closed on his right arm and crushed it to the bone. A moment later the dwarf, still clinging to his dog's back, thrust the point of his tiny sword into the body of the prostrate bareback rider.

Simon Lafleur struggled valiantly, but to no purpose. Now he felt the fetid breath of the dog fanning his neck and the wasp-like sting of the dwarf's blade, which this time found a mortal spot. A convulsive tremor shook him and he rolled over on his back. The circus Romeo was dead.

Monsieur Jacques Courbé cleansed his sword on a kerchief of lace, dismounted and approached Jeanne Marie. She was still crouching on the floor, her eyes closed, her head held tightly between both hands. The dwarf touched her imperiously on the broad shoulder which had so often carried him.

"Madame," he said, "we now can return home. You must be more careful hereafter. *Ma foi*, it is an ungentlemanly business cutting the throats of stable-boys!"

She rose to her feet, like a large trained animal at the word of command.

"You wish to be carried?" she said between livid lips.

"Ah, that is true, madame," he murmured. "I was forgetting our little wager. Ah, yes! Well, you are to be congratulated, madame—you have covered nearly half the distance."

"Nearly half the distance," she repeated in a lifeless voice.

"Yes, madame," Monsieur Jacques Courbé continued. "I fancy that you will be quite a docile wife by the time you have done." He paused and then added reflectively: "It is truly remarkable how speedily one can ride the devil out of a woman—with spurs!"

Papa Copo had been spending a convivial evening at the Sign of the Wild Boar. As he stepped out into the street he saw three familiar figures preceding him—a tall woman, a tiny man and a large dog with upstanding ears. The woman carried the man on her shoulder, the dog trotted at her heels.

The circus owner came to a halt and stared after them. His round eyes were full of childish astonishment.

"Can it be?" he murmured. "Yes, it is! Three old friends! And so Jeanne Marie still carries him! Ah, but she should not poke fun at Monsieur Jacques Courbé! He is so sensitive; but, alas, they are the kind that are always henpecked!"

www.ingramcontent.com/pod-product-compliance
Lightning Source LLC
Chambersburg PA
CBHW050311260626
47156CB00005B/1764

SIX MONTHS AGO, AMERICA DIED.

IS IT TOO SOON TO MAKE THE MOVIE?

A massive nuclear attack has destroyed the major cities. Untold millions are dead. The survivors are starving savages.

But where others see only tragedy, one man sees opportunity.

Enter Julian Harvey: an A-list producer with a hot project, a private army and a vision for America that will give her back her soul. It's the last Hollywood film crew, making the last Hollywood movie, in the radioactive crater formerly known as Los Angeles.

Spreading hope the only way they know how...through total bullshit.

And like it or not, you're along for the ride.

"Humor, heart, and wit so sharp you don't even know you're bleeding until after you've finished. I could not and did not put it down."
—Sarah Langan

"Packs a hell of a punch. Hilarious, savage and moving."
—Peter Tennant, Black Static

FUNGASM PRESS
205 NE BRYANT
PORTLAND, OR 97211

AN ERASERHEAD PRESS COMPANY
www.ERASERHEADPRESS.com

ISBN: 978-1-62105-090-2

The Last Goddam Hollywood Movie was previously released—in rougher, less radioactively-mutated form—as *The Day Before*: a far worse title that Julian Harvey, the authors, and Fungasm Press have wisely dispensed with in this new, improved Director's Cut!

Cover art and interior art copyright © 2013 Greg Houston
Cover design by Matthew Revert

Printed in the USA.